THE

MAGNIFICENT
MUMMIES

TONY BRADMAN
MARTIN CHATTERTON

Blue Bananas

Other titles in the bunch:

Big Dog and Little Dog Go Sailing
Big Dog and Little Dog Visit the Moon
Colin and the Curly Claw
Dexter's Journey
Follow the Swallow
"Here I Am!" said Smedley

Horrible Haircut
Magic Lemonade
The Magnificent Mummies
Midnight in Memphis
Peg
Shoot!

Crabtree Publishing Company
www.crabtreebooks.com

PMB 16A, 350 Fifth Avenue
Suite 3308
New York, NY 10118

612 Welland Avenue
St. Catharines, Ontario
Canada, L2M 5V6

Bradman, Tony.
   The Magnificent Mummies / Tony Bradman ; illustrated by
Martin Chatterton.
     p. cm. -- (Blue Bananas)
   Summary: When Sir Digby Digger shows up at the Mummy
Family's pyramid, their routine day becomes an adventure as they
help the archaeologist find new transportation and then need his
help to free a stuck whale.
     ISBN 0-7787-0843-8 -- ISBN 0-7787-0889-6 (pbk.)
    [1. Mummies--Fiction. 2. Humorous Stories.] I. Chatterton,
Martin, ill. II. Title. III. Series.
PZ7.B7275 Mag 2002
[E]--dc21

                    2001032438
                    LC

Published by Crabtree Publishing in 2002
First published in 1997 by Mammoth
an imprint of Egmont Children's Books Limited
Text copyright © Tony Bradman 1997
Illustrations copyright © Martin Chatterton 1997
The Author and Illustrator have asserted their moral rights.
Paperback ISBN 0-7787-0889-6
Reinforced Hardcover Binding ISBN 0-7787-0843-8

THE
MAGNIFICENT
MUMMIES

TONY BRADMAN
MARTIN CHATTERTON

Blue Bananas

For Bindi
T.B.

For Sophie and Danny
M.C.

Far away in the Land of Sand . . .

. . .there flows a big, slow river.

(Who's that swimming in it?

Oh, never mind.)

By that big, slow river,

there stands a pyramid.

(Who's that putting up a sign?

Oh, never mind.)

And inside that pyramid you'll find...

. . . a family of mummies.

And here they are to say hello!

The Mummies were having a quiet, restful day. Mommy Mummy was reading the paper. Daddy Mummy was cooking in the kitchen. The Mummy kids were watching TV.

11

The Mummy family sat down at the
table. Tut and Sis were soon
in trouble.

They were saved by a

loud knocking noise!

The knocking went on,

and on,

and on.

So the Mummies went to the front door.

Daddy Mummy opened the door and

the Mummies peered out.

A man was standing outside.

The man didn't say anything. He just went

very pale. . . and fainted on the ground.

They brought him in, and brought him around. The man soon got over his shock. His name was Sir Digby Digger. He was an archaeologist, so he did lots of digging. The Mummies asked Sir Digby to stay for dinner. They laughed and joked and became good friends.

But at last it was time

for Sir Digby to go.

The mummies gave Sir Digby some old

things they didn't need anymore.

He seemed quite pleased.

Then they took him

to the front door.

Sir Digby climbed into his car... but he

didn't get very far.

His car made an odd coughing noise.

Sir Digby's car just wouldn't start!

Sir Digby lost his temper.

Sir Digby kicked his car, very hard.

The Mummy family and Sir Digby tried
to fix the car. But it was no use.
All it did was cough, cough, cough.
Sir Digby was very upset.
He had an important appointment
at a monument in Memphis.
"It's at eight, and
I must not be late!"
said Sir Digby.

I'll be the mechanic!

Then Mommy Mummy

had a brilliant idea.

Mommy Mummy led the way.

They all went around the corner,

and around the corner again.

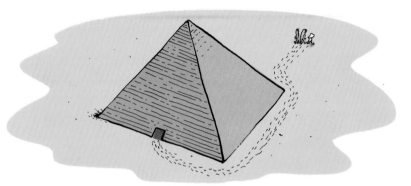

And there was the place Mommy

Mummy had read about in the paper.

The two guys were called Rattle and

Roll and they were very helpful.

Sir Digby chose a camel

and paid for it.

The camel left quite quickly.

The Mummies waved goodbye.

"What shall we do now?"

"The laundry, I think. You need some

clean bandages!" said Mommy Mummy.

So they
collected
the dirty
laundry
and headed
for the river.
But when
they arrived,
they couldn't
believe their
eyes. The
river had
vanished.
What a surprise!

The Mummies were stumped.

They stood on the sand of the river bank

and looked down at...more sand.

The Mummies set off to investigate.

Tut and Sis ran ahead.

But they soon came

racing back.

Tut and Sis were both very

excited. They dragged

Mommy Mummy and

Daddy Mummy

along by the hands.

And there it was. . .

The BIGGEST creature they

had ever seen.

It was a huge whale, and his name was Moby. He had become lost after swimming into the river by mistake. Now he was stuck tight where the river narrowed...

. . . and none of the water could flow past.

Poor Moby looked very unhappy.

Then Daddy Mummy had a fantastic

idea!

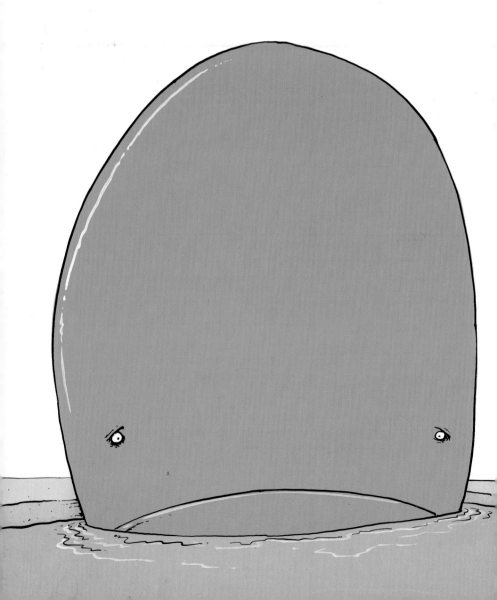

They needed someone who was

good at digging!

And they knew just the man for the job!

Daddy Mummy sent Tut and Sis

running off to the Used Camel

Lot with a message.

Minutes later a cloud of dust left

the pyramid.

Inside it were Tut and Sis.

Soon a much bigger cloud of dust

returned. Inside that cloud were Tut and

Sis, the two guys... and S̲ir Digby Digger!

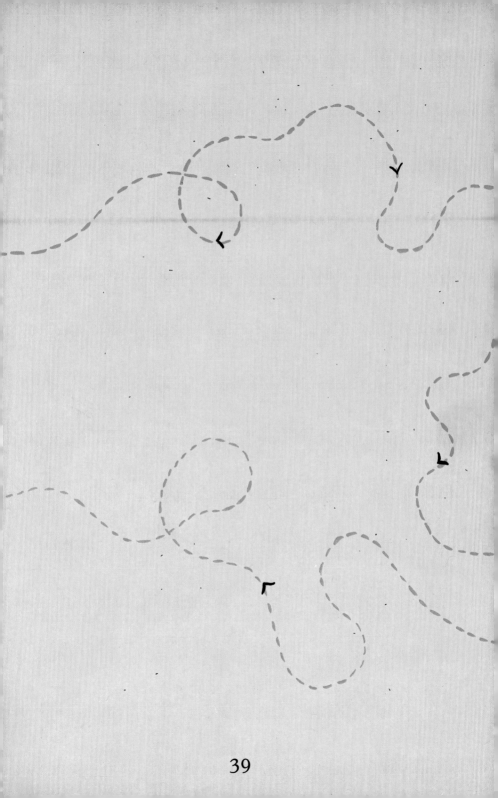

Sir Digby was a man with a plan.

He drew some lines in the sand . . .

and got everybody digging

and digging

and digging

The river came flooding back. And now there was a great big pool of lovely cool water, too. Moby was free!

He was very happy.

He made sure that Sir Digby and the two guys and the Mummies had a whale of a time!

The Mummies even got

the laundry done.

At last, the sun started to set,

and it was time to go.

Sir Digby left. . .

 the two guys left. . .

Moby left. . .

and the Mummy family left as well.

On the way home, they were so happy,

they did the famous Mummy sand

dance by the light of the moon.

I had been a wonderful day in the
Land of Sand.

And now the Mummies were very tired.

And that's the end of the story.